W9-AYM-683

King of the Mountain

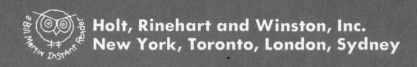

Holt, Rinehart and Winston, Inc.
New York, Toronto, London, Sydney

Copyright © 1970 by
Holt, Rinehart and Winston, Inc.
Published Simultaneously in Canada
Printed in the United States of America
Library of Congress Cat. No: 74-106417
SBN 03-084597-1

King of the Mountain

by Bill Martin Jr.

with pictures by Ivor Parry

It began to rain.

A boy looked out of the window and said,
"I'm the king of the puddle."

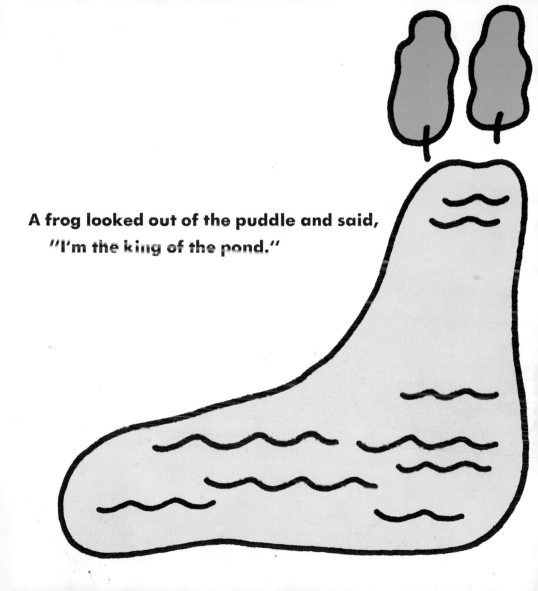

A frog looked out of the puddle and said,
"I'm the king of the pond."

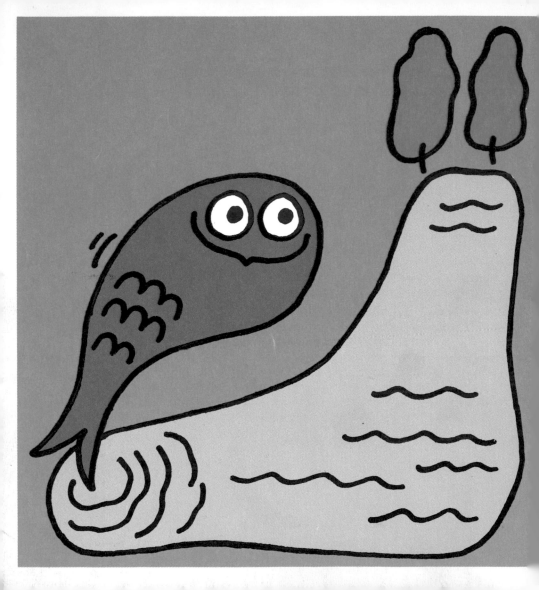

A minnow looked out of the pond and said,
"I'm the king of the lake."

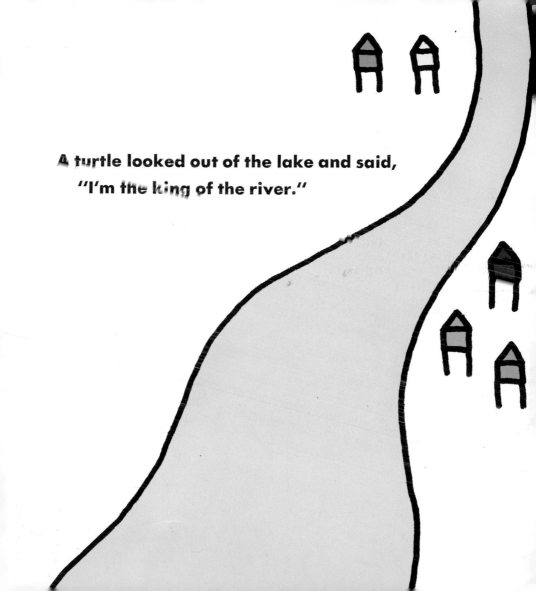

A turtle looked out of the lake and said,
"I'm the king of the river."

A crocodile looked out of the river and said,
"I'm the king of the ocean."

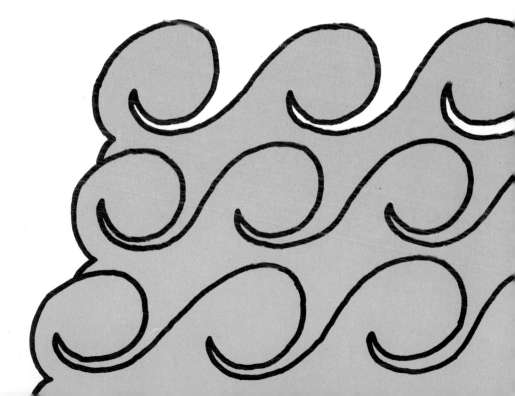

A whale looked out of the ocean and said,
"I'm the king of the mountain."

A dragon looked down from the mountain and said,
"I'm the king of the hilltops."

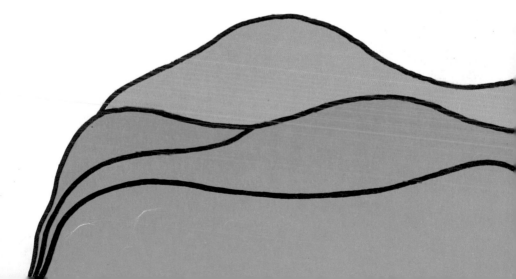

**A leopard looked down from the hilltops and said,
"I'm the king of the desert."**

**A camel looked over the desert and said,
"I'm the king of the grasslands."**

A lion looked out from the grasslands
and said,
"I'm the king of the jungle."

An elephant looked out of the jungle and said,
"I'm the king of the world."

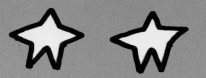

An astronaut looked down on the world and said,
"I'm the king of the universe."

A star looked down on the astronaut and said, "What on earth are they talking about?"

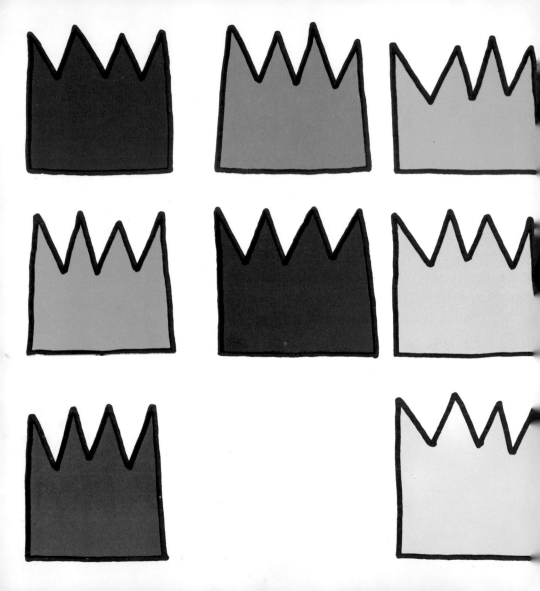